ST. MARY'S COLLEGE OF MARYLAND
ST. MARY'S CITY, MARYLAND

# NOCTURNES

# THOMAS MANN

# NOCTURNES
## WITH LITHOGRAPHS BY LYND WARD

*Short Story Index Reprint Series*

  BOOKS FOR LIBRARIES PRESS
FREEPORT, NEW YORK

First Published 1934
Reprinted 1970

INTERNATIONAL STANDARD BOOK NUMBER:
0-8369-3728-7

LIBRARY OF CONGRESS CATALOG CARD NUMBER:
79-140336

PRINTED IN THE UNITED STATES OF AMERICA

# A GLEAM

# A GLEAM

       Waltz time, tinkling glasses; smoke, steam, hubbub, voices, dance steps. We all know these little weaknesses of ours. Do we secretly love to linger at life's silliest feasts simply because there suffering wears bigger, more childlike eyes than in other places?

    "*Avantageur!*" cried Baron Harry, the cavalry captain. He stopped dancing and called the whole length of the hall, one hand on his hip, the other still holding his partner embraced. "That's not a waltz, man, it's a funeral march! You have no rhythm in your body; you just float and sway about without any sense of time. Let Lieutenant von Gelbsattel play, so that we can feel the rhythm. Come on down, *Avantageur!* Dance, if you can do that better!"

And the *Avantageur* stood up, clapped his spurs together and without a word yielded the platform to Lieutenant von Gelbsattel, who straightway began to make the piano ring and rattle under the blows from his sprawled-out white fingers.

Baron Harry, we observe, had music in him: waltz music, march music. He had rhythm, joviality, hauteur, good fortune and a conquering hero air. His gold-braided hussar jacket suited to a T his glowing young face, unmarked by a single care, a single thought. He was burnt red, like a blond, though hair and moustache were dark—a piquant combination that appealed to the ladies—and the red scar across his right cheek gave a bold and dashing look to his open countenance. The scar might be from a wound, or a fall from his horse—in any case it was glorious. He danced divinely.

But the *Avantageur* floated and swayed—to extend the meaning of Baron Harry's phrase. His eyelids were much too large, so that he could never properly open his eyes; also his uniform fitted him rather carelessly and improbably round the waist—and God alone knew how he came to be a soldier. He had not cared much for this affair with the "Swallows" at the Casino, but even so he had come to it; he had to be careful not to give offence, for two reasons: first, because his origins were bourgeois, and second, because there was a book by him, that he had written or put together, or whatever the word is, a collection of stories, that anybody could buy in a book-shop. It must make people feel a little shy of him, of course.

The hall in the officers' casino was long and wide—much too large for the thirty people who were disporting themselves in it. The walls and the musicians' platform were decorated with imitation draperies in red plaster, and from the ugly ceiling hung two crooked chandeliers, in which the candles stood askew and dripped hot wax. But the board floor had been scrubbed the whole forenoon by seven hussars told off for the job; and after all, officers in a little hole like Hohendamm could not expect grandeur. Whatever was otherwise lacking to the feast was amply made up by its characteristic atmosphere; it had the sweetness of forbidden fruit, the reckless charm imparted by the presence of the "Swallows." Even the orderlies smirked knowingly, as they renewed the supplies of champagne in the ice-tubs beside the white-covered tables which stood ranged along three walls of the room. They looked at each other and then down with a grin, as servants do when they assist irresponsibly at the excesses of their masters. And all this with reference to the "Swallows."

The Swallows, the Swallows? Well, in short, they were the "Swallows from Vienna." Like migratory birds, thirty in the flock, they flew through the country, appearing in fifth-rate variety-theatres and music-halls, where they stood on the stage in easy, unconventional poses and chirped their renowned swallows' chorus:

> "When the swallows come again
> See them fly, *aren't* they fly?"

It was a good song, its humor was not obscure; it was always received with warm applause from the more knowing section of the public.

Well, the Swallows came to Hohendamm, and sang in Gugelfing's beer-hall. A whole regiment of hussars were in barracks at Hohendamm, and the Swallows were justified in anticipating a good reception from representative circles. But they got more, they got an enthusiastic one. Evening after evening the unmarried officers sat at the girls' feet, listened to their swallow song and drank their health in Gugelfing's yellow beer. It was not long before the married officers were there too; one evening Colonel von Rummler appeared in person, followed the programme with the closest interest and afterwards expressed himself with unlimited approval in various places.

So then the lieutenants and cavalry captains conceived a plan to bring about closer contact with the Swallows: to invite a select group of them, say, ten of the prettiest, to a jolly champagne supper in the Casino. The upper orders could not take any public cognizance of the affair, of course; they had to refrain, however sore at heart. Not only the unmarried lieutenants, however, but also the married first lieutenants and cavalry captains took part, and also—this was the nub of the whole matter, the thing that gave it, so to speak, its "punch"—their wives.

Obstacles and misgivings? First Lieutenant von Levzahn brushed them all away with a phrase: what else, said he, were obstacles for, if not that soldiers might triumph over them! The good citizens of Hohendamm might rage, when they heard that the officers were introducing their wives to the Swallows. Of course, they could not have done such a thing themselves. But there were heights, there were aloof and untrammelled regions of existence, where things might freely come to pass that in a lower sphere could only sully and dishonor. It was not as though the worthy natives of Hohendamm were not used to expecting all sorts of unexpectednesses from their hussars. The officers would ride along the middle of the sidewalk, in broad daylight, if it occurred to them so to do. They had done it. One evening, pistols had been fired off in the Marktplatz—nobody but the officers could have done that. And had anyone dared to murmur? The following anecdote was amply vouched for:

One morning, between five and six o'clock, Captain of Cavalry Baron Harry, feeling pretty jolly, was on his way home from a party, with his friends, Captain of Cavalry von Hühnemann and Lieutenants Le Maistre, Baron Truchsess, von Trautenau and von Lichterloh. Riding across the Old Bridge, they met a baker's boy, with a great basket of rolls on his shoulder, taking his way through the fresh morning air and whistling blithely as he went. "Give me that basket!" commanded Baron Harry. He seized it by the handle, swung it three times round his head, so skilfully that not a roll fell out, and sent it flying out into the stream on a great curve that showed the strength of his arm. At first the baker's boy was scared stiff. Then as he saw his rolls swimming about he flung up his arms with a yell and behaved as though he had gone out of his mind. The gentlemen amused themselves for a while with his childish despair; then Baron Harry tossed him a gold piece which would have paid three times over for his loss and the officers rode laughing away home. Then the boy realized that these were the nobility, and ceased his outcry.

This story lost no time in going the rounds—but who would have ventured to look askance? You might gnash your teeth over the pranks of Baron Harry and his friends; outwardly you took them with a smile. They were the lords and masters of Hohendamm, And now the lords and masters were having a party for the Swallows.

The *Avantageur* seemed not to know how to dance a waltz any better than to play one. For he did not take a partner, but going up to one of the little white tables made a bow and sat down near little Baroness Anna, Baron Harry's wife, to whom he addressed a few shy words. The capacity to amuse himself with a Swallow was simply beyond the poor young man. Actually he was afraid of that kind of girl; he fancied that whatever he said to one she looked at him as though she were surprised—and this hurt the *Avantageur*. But music, even the poorest, always put him into a speechless, relaxed and dreamy mood—it is often the way with these flabby and futile characters; and as the Baroness Anna, to whom he was entirely indifferent, made only absent answers to his remarks, they soon fell silent, and confined themselves to gazing into the whirling scene, with the same somewhat wry smile, strange to say, on both their faces.

☆                                  A GLEAM

The candles flickered and sputtered so much that they became quite misshapen with great blobs of soft wax. Beneath them the couples twisted and turned in obedience to Lieutenant von Gelbsattel's inspiring strains. They put out their feet and pointed their toes, swung round with a flourish, then glided away. The gentlemen's long legs bent and balanced and sprang again. Petticoats flew. Gay hussar jackets whirled in abandon; voluptuously the ladies inclined their heads, yielding their waists to their partners' embraces.

Baron Harry held an amazingly pretty young Swallow pressed fairly close to his braided chest, putting his face down to hers and looking unswervingly into her eyes. Baroness Anna's gaze and her smile followed the pair. The long, lanky Lichterloh was trundling along with a plump and dumpy little Swallow in an extraordinary décolletage. But Frau Cavalry Captain von Hühnemann, who loved champagne above all else in life, there she was, dancing round and round under one of the chandeliers, completely absorbed, with another Swallow, a friendly creature whose freckled face beamed all over at the unprecedented honor done her. "My dear Baroness," Frau von Hühnemann said later to Frau First Lieutenant von Truchsess, "these girls are far from being ignorant. They know all the cavalry garrisons in Germany off by heart."

# NOCTURNES ☆ ☆

The pair were dancing together because there were two extra ladies; they were quite unaware that the other couples had gradually left the field to them, until they were performing all by themselves. At last, however, they saw what had happened, and stood there together in the center of the hall, overwhelmed from all sides by laughter and applause.

Next came the champagne, and the white-gloved orderlies ran from table to table pouring out. After that the Swallows were urged to sing again—they simply had to sing, no matter how out of breath they were.

They stood on the platform that ran along the narrow side of the hall, and made eyes at the company. Their shoulders and arms were bare, and they were dressed like the birds they represented, in long dark swallow-tails over pale grey waistcoats. They wore grey clocked stockings and slippers with very low vamps and very high heels. There were blonde and brunette, there were the fat, good-natured and the interestingly lean; there were some whose cheeks were staringly rouged, others with faces chalk-white like clowns. But the prettiest was the little dark one who had almond-shaped eyes and arms like a child's —she it was with whom Baron Harry had just danced. Baroness Anna too found that she was the prettiest one, and continued to smile.

☆ **A GLEAM**

The Swallows sang, and Lieutenant von Gelbsattel accompanied them, flinging back his torso and twisting round his head to look, while his long arms reached out after the keys. They sang as with one voice, that they were gay birds, that they had flown the world over and always left broken hearts behind them when they flew away. They sang another very tuneful piece beginning

"Yes, yes, the arm-y,
How we love the arm-y"

and ending with the same. And in response to vociferous requests they repeated their Swallow song, and the officers who knew it by now as well as they did, joined lustily in the chorus:

"When the swallows come again
See them fly—*aren't* they fly?"

The whole hall rang with laughter and song and the stamping and clinking of spurred feet beating out the time.

Baroness Anna laughed too, at all the nonsense and extravagant spirits. She had laughed so much already, all the evening, that her head and her heart ached, and she would have been glad to close her eyes in darkness and quiet, had not Harry been so zealous in his pleasures. "I feel so jolly today," she had told her neighbor, at a moment when she believed what she said; but the neighbor had answered only by a mocking look, and she had realized that people do not say such things. If you really feel jolly, you act like it; to proclaim the fact makes it sound queer. On the other hand, it would have been quite impossible to say, "I feel so sad!"

Baroness Anna had grown up in the solitude and stillness of her father's estate by the sea; she was at all times too much inclined to leave out of consideration such home truths as the above, despite her constitutional fear of putting people out and her constitutional yearning to be like them and have them love her. She had white hands and heavy, ash-blond hair—much too heavy for her narrow face with its delicate bones. Between her light eye-brows ran a perpendicular furrow, which gave a pained expression to her smile.

The truth was, she loved her husband. You must not laugh. She loved him even for the prank with the rolls. With a cowering and miserable love, though he betrayed her and daily abused her love like a schoolboy. She suffered for love of him as a woman does who despises her own weak tenderness and knows that power and the happiness of the powerful are justified on this earth. Yes, she yielded herself to love and its torments as once she had yielded herself to him, when in a brief attack of tenderness he wooed her; with the hungry yearning of a lonely and dreamy soul, that craves for life and passion and an outlet for its emotions.

Waltz time, tinkling glasses—hurly-burly and smoke, voices and dancing steps. That was Harry's world, and his kingdom. It was the kingdom of her dreams as well: the world of love and life, the happy commonplace.

Social life, harmless, jolly conviviality—what a frightful thing it is, how enervating, how degrading; what a vain, alluring poison, what an insidious enemy to our peace. There she sat, evening after evening, night after night, a martyr to the glaring contrast between the utter emptiness round about her and the feverish excitement born of wine and coffee, of sensual music and the dance. She sat and looked on while Harry exercised his arts of fascination upon gay and pretty ladies—not because of their personal charms but because it fed his vanity to have people see him with them and know what a lucky man he was, how much in the center of things, without one single ungratified longing. His vanity hurt her—and yet, she loved it! How sweet to feel how handsome he was, how young, splendid and bewitching! The infatuation of those other women would bring her own to fever pitch. And when afterwards, at the end of an evening spent by her in suffering for his sake, he would exhaust himself in stupid and self-centered expressions of enjoyment, there would come moments when her hatred and scorn outweighed her love; in her heart she would call him a puppy and a trifler and try to punish him by not talking, by an absurd and desperate dumbness.

Are we guessing right, little Baroness Anna? Are we giving words to all that lay behind that poor little smile of yours, as the Swallows sang their song? Behind that pitiable and shameful state, when you lay in bed afterwards in the grey dawn, thinking of the jests, the witticisms, the repartee, the social charms you should have displayed—and did not! Dreams come, in that grey dawn: you, quite worn with anguish, weep on his shoulder, he tries to console you with some of his empty, pleasant, commonplace phrases and you are suddenly overcome with the mockery of your situation: you, lying on his shoulder, are shedding tears over the whole world!

Suppose he were to fall ill? Are we right in saying that some small trifling indisposition of his could call up a whole world of dreams for you, wherein you see him as your ailing child; in which he lies helpless and broken before you, and at last, at last, belongs to you alone? Do not blush, do not shrink away! Trouble does sometimes make us think bad thoughts. But after all you might trouble yourself a little about the young *Avantageur* with the drooping eyelids, sitting there beside you—how gladly he would share his loneliness with you! Why do you scorn him? Why despise? Because he belongs to your own world, not to that other where pride and high spirits reign, and conscious triumph and dancing rhythm. Truly it is hard, not to be at home in one world or in the other. We know. But there is no halfway house.

Applause broke in upon Lieutenant von Gelbsattel's final chords. The Swallows had finished their song. They scorned the steps of the platform and jumped down from the front, flopping or fluttering—the gentlemen rushed up to be of help. Baron Harry helped the little brunette Swallow with the childlike arms; he helped her very efficiently and with understanding for such things. He took her by the thigh and the waist, gave himself plenty of time to set her down, then almost carried her to the table, where he brimmed her glass with champagne till it overflowed and touched his own to it, slowly, meaningfully, gazing into her eyes with a foolish, insistent smile. He had drunk a good deal, and the scar stood out on his forehead, that looked very white next his glowing face. But his mood was a free and hilarious one, unclouded by any passion.

His table stood opposite to Baroness Anna's across the

hall. As she sat talking idly with her neighbor she was listening greedily to the laughter over there, and sending stolen and reproachful glances to watch every moment—in that painful state of tension which enables a person to carry on a conversation that complies with all the social forms, while actually being elsewhere all the time, and in the presence of the person one is watching.

Once or twice it seemed to her that the little Swallow's eye caught her own. Did she know her? Did she know who she was? How lovely she looked! How provocative, how full of fascination and thoughtless life! If Harry were in love with her, if he burned and suffered for her sake, his wife could have forgiven that, she could have understood and sympathized. And suddenly she became conscious that her own feeling for the little Swallow was warmer and deeper than Harry's own.

And the little Swallow herself? Dear me, her name was Emmy, and she was fundamentally commonplace. But she was wonderful too, with black strands of hair framing a wide, sensuous face, shadowed, almond-shaped eyes, a generous mouth full of shining teeth, and those arms like a child's. Loveliest of all were the shoulders—they had a way of moving with such ineffable suppleness in their sockets. Baron Harry took great interest in these shoulders; he would not have them covered, and set up a noisy struggle for the scarf which she would have put about them. And in all this, nobody in the whole hall saw, neither Baron Harry nor his wife nor anyone else, that this poor little waif, made sentimental by the wine she had drunk, had all the evening been casting longing glances at the young *Avantageur* whose lack of feeling for rhythm had caused his demission from the piano-stool. She had been drawn by the way he played, by his drooping lids, she found him noble, poetic, a being from a different world—whereas she was familiar unto boredom with Baron Harry's sort and all its works and ways. She was saddened, she was wretched, because the *Avantageur* cast not a thought in her direction.

The candles burned low and dim in the cigarette smoke and blue wreaths drifted above the company's heads. There was a smell of coffee on the heavy air, and odors and vapors of the feast, made still more heady by the somewhat daring perfume affected by the Swallows, hung about the scene; the white tables and champagne coolers, the men and women, flirting, giggling and guffawing, weary-eyed and unrestrained.

Baroness Anna talked no more. Despair—and that frightful mixture of yearning, envy, love and self-contempt which we call jealousy, and which makes the world no good place at all to live in—had so subdued her heart that she had not power to counterfeit any more. Let him see how she felt, perhaps he would be ashamed—or at least, he would have some feeling about her, of whatever kind, in his heart.

She looked across. The game over there was going rather far, everybody was watching and laughing. Harry had thought of a new kind of amorous struggle with the fair Swallow: it consisted in an exchange of rings. Bracing his knee against hers he held her fast to her chair, and snatched and tugged after her hand in a violent effort to open her little clenched fist. In the end he won. Amid noisy applause he wrenched off the narrow circlet she wore—it cost him some trouble—and triumphantly forced his own wedding ring upon her finger.

Then Baroness Anna stood up. Anger and pain, a longing to hide herself away in the dark with her sense of his so dear unworthiness; a desperate desire to punish him by making a scandal, by forcing him at all costs to acknowledge her presence—such were the emotions that overpowered her. She pushed back her chair, and pale as death she walked across the hall towards the door.

There was a great sensation. People were sobered, they looked at one another grave-faced. One or two gentlemen called out Harry's name. It became suddenly still in the hall.

Then something very odd happened: the little Swallow —Emmy—suddenly and decisively espoused the Baroness' cause. Perhaps she was moved by a natural feminine instinct of pity for suffering love; perhaps her own pangs for the *Avantageur* with the drooping lids made her see in the little Baroness a fellow-sufferer. In any case, she acted—to the amazement of the company.

"You are coarse!" she said loudly, in the hush, and gave the dumbfounded Harry a great push. Just these three words: You are coarse. And all at once she was at Baroness Anna's side, where the latter stood lifting the latch of the door.

"Forgive!" she breathed—softly, as though no one else in the room were worthy to hear. "Here is the ring," and she slipped Harry's wedding-ring into the Baroness' hand. And suddenly Baroness Anna felt the girl's broad, glowing face bend over this hand of hers; she felt burning on it a soft and passionate kiss. "Forgive!" whispered the little Swallow once more, and ran off.

But Baroness Anna stood outside in the darkness, still quite dazed, and waited for this unexpected event to take on shape and meaning within her. And it did: it was a joy, so warm, so sweet, so comfortable that for a moment she closed her eyes.

We stop here. No more, it is enough. Just this one priceless little detail, as it stands: there she was, quite enraptured and enchanted, simply because this little chit of a strolling chorus-girl had come and kissed her hand!

We leave you, Baroness Anna. We kiss your brow and take our leave; farewell, we must hurry away. Sleep, now. You will dream all night of the Swallow who came to you, and you will have a gleam of happiness.

For it brings happiness, it brings to the heart a little thrill and ecstasy of joy, when two worlds, between which longing plies, for one fleeting, illusory moment touch each other.

# RAILWAY ACCIDENT

# RAILWAY ACCIDENT

Tell you a story? But I don't know any. Well, yes, after all, here is something I might tell.

Once, two years ago now it is, I was in a railway accident; all the details are clear in my memory.

It was not really a first-class one—no wholesale telescoping or "heaps of unidentifiable dead"—not that sort of thing. Still, it was a proper accident, with all the trimmings, and on top of that it was at night. Not everybody has been through one, so I will describe it the best I can.

I was on my way to Dresden, whither I had been invited by some friends of letters: it was a literary and artistic pilgrimage, in short, such as, from time to time, I undertake not unwillingly. You make appearances, you attend functions, you show yourself to admiring crowds— not for nothing is one a subject of William II. And certainly Dresden is beautiful, especially the Zwinger; and afterwards I intended to go for ten days or a fortnight to the White Hart to rest, and if, thanks to the treatments, the spirit should come upon me, I might do a little work as well. To this end I had put my manuscript at the bottom of my trunk, together with my notes—a good stout bundle done up in brown paper and tied with string in the Bavarian colors. I like to travel in comfort, especially when my expenses are paid. So I patronized the sleeping-cars, reserving a place days ahead in a first-class compartment. All was in order; nevertheless I was excited, as I always am on such occasions, for a journey is still an adventure to me, and where travelling is concerned I shall never manage to feel properly blasé. I perfectly well know that the night train for Dresden leaves the central station at Munich regularly every evening and every morning is in Dresden. But when I am travelling with it, and linking my momentous destiny to its own, the matter assumes importance. I cannot rid myself of the notion that it is making a special trip today, just on my account, and the unreasoning and mistaken conviction sets up in me a deep and speechless unrest, which does not subside until all the formalities of departure are behind me—the packing, the drive in the loaded cab to the station, the arrival there and the registration of luggage—and I can feel myself finally and securely bestowed. Then, indeed, a pleasing relaxation takes place, the mind turns to fresh concerns, the unknown unfolds itself beyond the expanse of window-pane, and I am consumed with joyful anticipations.

And so on this occasion. I had tipped my porter so liberally that he pulled his cap and gave me a pleasant journey; and I stood at the corridor window of my sleeping-car smoking my evening cigar and watching the bustle on the platform. There were whistlings and rumblings, hurryings and farewells and the sing-song of newspaper and refreshment vendors, and over all the great electric moons glowed through the mist of the October evening. Two stout fellows pulled a handcart of large trunks along the platform to the baggage car in front of the train. I easily identified, by certain unmistakable features, my own trunk; one among many there it lay, and at the bottom of it reposed my precious package. "There," thought I, "no need to worry, it is in good hands. Look at that guard with the leather cartridge belt, the prodigious sergeant-major's moustache and the inhospitable eye. Watch him rebuking the old woman in the threadbare black cape—for two pins she would have got into a second-class carriage. He is security, he is authority, he is our parent, he is the State. He is strict, not to say rude, you would not care to mingle with him; but reliability is writ large upon his brow, and in his care your trunk reposes as in the bosom of Abraham."

A man was strolling up and down the platform in spats and a yellow autumn coat, with a dog on a leash. Never have I seen a handsomer dog, a small, stocky bull, smooth-coated, muscular, with black spots; as well groomed and amusing as the dogs one sees in circuses, who make the audience laugh by dashing round and round the ring with all the energy of their small bodies. This dog had a silver collar, with a plaited leather leash. But all this was not surprising, considering his master, the gentleman in spats, who had beyond a doubt the noblest origins. He wore a monocle, which accentuated without distorting his general air; the defiant perch of his moustache bore out the proud and stubborn expression of his chin and the corners of his mouth. He addressed a question to the martial guard, who knew perfectly well with whom he was dealing and answered hand to cap. My gentleman strolled on, gratified with the impression he had made. He strutted in his spats, his gaze was cold, he regarded men and affairs with penetrating eye. Certainly he was far above feeling journey-proud; travel by train was no novelty to him. He was at home in life, without fear of authority or regulations; he was an authority himself—in short, a nob. I could not look at him enough. When he thought the time had come, he got into the train (the guard had just turned his back). He went along the corridor behind me, bumped into me and did not apologize. What a man! But that was nothing to what followed. Without turning a hair he took his dog with him into the sleeping-compartment! Surely it was forbidden to do that. When should I presume to take a dog with me into a sleeping-compartment? But he did it, on the strength of his prescriptive rights as a nob, and shut the door behind him.

There came a whistle outside, the locomotive whistled in response, gently the train began to move. I stayed a while by the window watching the hand-waving and shifting lights. . . . I retired inside the carriage.

The sleeping-car was not very full, a compartment next to mine was empty and had not been got ready for the night; I decided to make myself comfortable there for an hour's peaceful reading. I fetched my book and settled in. The sofa had a silky salmon-pink covering, an ashtray stood on the folding-table, the light burned bright. I read and smoked.

# RAILWAY ACCIDENT

The sleeping-car attendant entered in pursuance of his duties and asked for my ticket for the night. I delivered it into his grimy hands. He was polite but entirely official, did not even vouchsafe me a good-night as from one human being to another, but went out at once and knocked on the door of the next compartment. He would better have left it alone, for my gentleman of the spats was inside; and perhaps because he did not wish anyone to discover his dog, but possibly because he had really gone to bed, he got furious at anyone daring to disturb him. Above the rumbling of the train I heard his immediate and elemental burst of rage. "What do you want?" he roared. "Leave me alone, you swine." He said swine. It was a lordly epithet, the epithet of a cavalry officer—it did my heart good to hear it. But the sleeping-car attendant must have resorted to diplomacy—of course he had to have the man's ticket—for just as I stepped into the corridor to get a better view the door of the compartment abruptly opened a little way and the ticket flew out into the attendant's face; yes, it was flung with violence straight in his face. He picked it up with both hands, and though he had got the corner of it in one eye, so that the tears came, he thanked the man, saluting and clicking his heels together. Quite overcome, I returned to my book.

I considered whether there was anything against my

# NOCTURNES ☆ ☆

smoking another cigar and concluded that there was little or nothing. So I did it, rolling onward and reading; I felt full of contentment and good ideas. Time passed, it was ten o'clock, half past ten, all my fellow-travellers had gone to bed, at last I decided to follow them. I got up and went into my own compartment. A real little bedroom, most luxurious, with stamped leather wall hangings, clothes hooks, a nickel-plated wash-basin. The lower-berth was snowily prepared, the covers invitingly turned back. O triumph of modern times! I thought. One lies in this bed as though at home, it rocks a little all night and the result is that next morning one is in Dresden. I took my suitcase out of the rack to get ready for bed; I was holding it above my head, with my arms stretched up.

It was at this moment that the railway accident occurred. I remember it like yesterday.

We gave a jerk—but jerk is a poor word for it. It was a jerk of deliberately foul intent, a jerk with a horrid reverberating crash, and so violent that my suitcase leaped out of my hands I knew not whither, while I was flung forcibly with my shoulder against the wall. I had no time to stop and think. But now followed a frightful rocking of the carriage, and while that went on one had plenty of leisure to be frightened. A railway carriage rocks going over switches or on sharp curves, that we know; but this rocking would not let me stand up, I was thrown from one wall to the other as the carriage careened. I had only one simple thought, but I thought it with concentration, exclusively. I thought, "Something is the matter, something is the matter, something is *very much* the matter!" Just in those words. But later I thought, "Stop, stop, stop!" For I knew that it would be a great help if only the train could be brought to a halt. And lo, at this my unuttered but fervent behest the train did stop.

Up to now a deathlike stillness had reigned in the carriage, but at this point terror found tongue. Shrill feminine screams mingled with deeper masculine cries of alarm. Next door someone was shouting "Help!" No doubt about it, this was the very same voice which, just previously, had uttered the lordly epithet—the voice of the man in spats, his very voice, though distorted by fear. "Help!" it cried; and just as I stepped into the corridor where the passengers were collecting, he burst out of his compartment in a silk sleeping-suit, and halted, looking wildly round him. "Great God!" he exclaimed, "Almighty God!" and then, as though to abase himself utterly, perhaps in hope to avert destruction, he added in a deprecating tone, *"Dear* God!" But suddenly he thought of something else, of trying to help himself. He threw himself upon the case on the wall where an axe and saw are kept for emergencies, and broke the glass with his fist. But finding that he could not release the tools at once he abandoned them, buffeted his way through the crowd of passengers, so that the half-dressed women screamed afresh, and leaped out of the carriage.

All that was the work of a moment only. And then for the first time I began to feel the shock: in a certain weakness of the spine, a passing inability to swallow. The sleeping-car attendant, red-eyed, grimy-handed, had just come up, we all pressed round him; the women, with bare arms and shoulders, stood wringing their hands.

The train, he explained, had been derailed, we had run off the track. That, as it afterwards turned out, was not true. But behold, the man in his excitement had become voluble, he abandoned his official neutrality; events had loosened his tongue and he spoke to us in confidence, about his wife. "I told her today, I did. 'Wife,' I said, 'I feel in my bones somethin's goin' to happen'." And sure enough, hadn't something happened? We all felt how right he had been. The carriage had begun to fill with smoke, a thick smudge; nobody knew where it came from, but we all thought it best to get out into the night.

That could only be done by quite a big jump from the footboard on to the track, for there was no platform of course, and besides our carriage was canted a good deal

# RAILWAY ACCIDENT

toward the opposite side. But the ladies—they had hastily covered their nakedness—jumped in desperation and soon we were all standing there between the tracks.

It was nearly dark, but from where we were we could see that no damage had been done at the rear of the train, though all the carriages stood at a slant. But further forward—fifteen or twenty paces further forward! Not for nothing had the jerk we felt made such a horrid crash. There lay a waste of wreckage; we could see the margins of it, with the little lights of the guards' lanterns flickering across and to and fro.

Excited people came toward us, bringing reports of the situation. We were close by a small station not far beyond Regensburg, and as the result of a defective point our express had run on to the wrong line, had crashed at full speed into a stationary freight train, hurling it out of the station, annihilating its rear carriages and itself sustaining serious damage. The great express engine from Maffei's in Munich lay smashed up and done for. Price seventy thousand marks. And in the forward coaches, themselves lying almost on one side, many of the seats were telescoped. No, thank goodness, there were no lives lost. There was talk of an old woman having been "taken out" but nobody had seen her. At least, people had been thrown in all directions, children buried under luggage, the shock had been great. The baggage car was demolished. Demolished—the baggage car? Demolished.

There I stood.

A bareheaded official came running along the track. The station master. He issued wild and tearful commands to the passengers, to make them behave themselves and get back into the coaches. But nobody took any notice of him, he had no cap and no self-control. Poor wretch! Probably the responsibility was his. Perhaps this was the end of his career, the wreck of his prospects. I could not ask him about the baggage car—it would have been tactless.

Another official came up—he *limped* up. I recognized him by the sergeant-major's moustache: it was the stern and vigilant guard of the early evening—our Father, the State. He limped along, bent over with his hand on his knee, thinking about nothing else. "Oh, dear!" he said, "Oh, dear, oh, dear me!" I asked him what was the matter. "I got stuck, sir, jammed me in the chest, I made my escape through the roof." This "made my escape through the roof" sounded like a newspaper report. Certainly the man would not have used the phrase in everyday life; he had experienced not so much an accident as a newspaper account of it—but what was that to me? He was in no state to give me news of my manuscript. So I accosted a young man who came up bustling and self-important from the waste of wreckage, and asked him about the heavy luggage.

"Well, sir, nobody can say anything as to that"—his tone implied that I ought to be grateful to have escaped unhurt. "Everything is all over the place. Women's shoes . . . " he said with a sweeping gesture to indicate the devastation, and wrinkled his nose. "When they start the clearing operations we shall see . . . Women's shoes. . . ."

There I stood. All alone I stood there in the night and searched my heart. Clearing operations. Clearing operations were to be undertaken with my manuscript. Probably it was destroyed, then, torn up, demolished. My honeycomb, my spider-web, my nest, my earth, my pride and pain, my all, the best of me—what should I do if it were gone? I had no copy of what had been welded and forged, of what already was a living, speaking thing—to say nothing of my notes and drafts, all that I had saved and stored up and overheard and sweated over for years—my squirrel's hoard. What should I do? I inquired of my own soul and I knew that I should begin over again from the beginning. Yes, with animal patience, with the tenacity of a primitive creature the curious and complex product of whose little ingenuity and industry has been destroyed, after a moment of helpless bewilderment I should set to work again—and perhaps this time it would come easier!

But meanwhile a fire brigade had come up, their torches cast a red light over the wreck; when I went forward and looked for the baggage car, behold it was almost intact, the luggage quite unharmed. All the things that lay strewn about came out of the freight train: among the rest a quantity of balls of string—a perfect sea of string covered the ground far and wide.

A load was lifted from my heart. I mingled with the people who stood talking and fraternizing in misfortune —also showing off and being important. So much seemed clear, that the engine-driver had acted with great presence of mind. He had averted a great catastrophe by pulling the emergency brake at the last moment. Otherwise, it was said, there would have been a general smash and the whole train would have gone over the steep embankment on the left. O praiseworthy engine-driver! He was not about, nobody had seen him, but his fame spread down the whole length of the train and we all lauded him in his absence. "That chap," said one man, and pointed with one hand somewhere off into the night, "that chap saved our lives." We all agreed.

But our train was standing on a track where it did not belong, and it behooved those in charge to guard it from behind so that another one did not run into it. Firemen

# RAILWAY ACCIDENT

perched on the rear carriage with torches of flaming pitch, and the excited young man who had given me such a fright with his "women's shoes" seized upon a torch too and began signalling with it, though no train was anywhere in sight.

Slowly and by degrees something like order was produced, the State our Father regained poise and presence. Steps had been taken, wires sent, presently a breakdown train from Regensburg steamed cautiously into the station and great gas flares with reflectors were set up about the wreck. We passengers were now turned off and told to go into the little station building to wait for our new conveyance. Laden with our hand luggage, some of the party with bandaged heads, we passed through a lane of inquisitive natives into the tiny waiting-room, where we herded together as best we could. And inside of an hour we were all stowed higgledy-piggledy into a special train.

I had my first-class ticket—my journey being paid for—but it availed me nothing, for everybody wanted to ride first and my carriage was more crowded than the others. But just as I found me a little niche, whom do I see diagonally opposite to me, huddled in the corner? My hero, the gentleman with the spats and the vocabulary of a cavalry officer. He did not have his dog, it had been taken away from him in defiance of his rights as a nob, and now sat howling in a gloomy prison just behind the engine. His master, like myself, held a yellow ticket which was no good to him, and he was grumbling, he was trying to make head against this communistic levelling of rank in the face of general misfortune. But another man answered him in a virtuous tone: "You ought to be thankful that you can sit down." And with a sour smile my gentleman resigned himself to the crazy situation.

And now who got in, supported by two firemen? A wee little old grandmother in a tattered black cape, the very same who in Munich would for two pins have got into a second class carriage. "Is this the first class?" she kept asking. And when we made room and assured her that it was, she sank down with a "God be praised!" on to the plush cushions as though only now was she safe and sound.

By Hof it was already five o'clock and light. There we breakfasted, an express train picked me up and deposited me with my belongings, three hours late, in Dresden.

Well, that was the railway accident I went through. I suppose it had to happen once; but whatever mathematicians may say, I feel that I now have every chance of escaping another.

# A WEARY HOUR

# A WEARY HOUR

He got up from the table, his little, fragile writing desk; got up as though desperate, and with hanging head crossed the room to the tall, thin, pillar-like stove in the opposite corner. He put his hands to it; but the hour was long past midnight and the tiles were nearly stone cold. Not getting even this little comfort that he sought, he leaned his back against them, and coughing drew together the folds of his dressing-gown, between which a draggled lace shirt-frill stuck out; he snuffed hard through his nostrils to get a little air, for as usual he had a cold.

It was a particular, a sinister cold, which scarcely ever quite disappeared. It inflamed his eyelids and made the flanges of his nose all raw; in his head and limbs it lay like a heavy, somber intoxication. Or was this cursed confinement to his room, to which the doctor had weeks ago condemned him, to blame for all his languor and flabbiness? God knew if it was the right thing—perhaps so, on account of his chronic catarrh and the spasms in his chest and belly. And for weeks on end now, yes, weeks, bad weather had reigned in Jena—hateful, horrible weather, which he felt in every nerve of his body—cold, wild, gloomy. The December wind roared in the stove-pipe with a desolate god-forsaken sound—he might have been wandering on a heath, by night and storm, his soul full of unappeasable grief. Yet this close confinement—that was not good either; not good for thought, nor for the rhythm of the blood, where thought was engendered.

The six-sided room was bare and colorless and devoid of cheer: a white-washed ceiling wreathed in tobacco smoke, walls covered with trellis-patterned paper and hung with silhouettes in oval frames, half a dozen slender-legged pieces of furniture; the whole lighted by two candles burning at the head of the manuscript on the writing-table. Red curtains draped the upper part of the window frames; mere festooned wisps of cotton they were, but red, a warm, sonorous red, and he loved them and would not have parted from them; they gave a little air of ease and charm to the bald unlovely poverty of his surroundings. He stood by the stove and blinked repeatedly, straining his eyes across at the work from which he had just fled: that load, that weight, that gnawing conscience, that sea which to drink up, that frightful task which to perform, was all his pride and all his misery, at once his heaven and his hell. It dragged, it stuck, it would not budge—and now again . . . ! It must be the weather; or his catarrh, or his fatigue. Or was it the work? Was the thing itself an unfortunate conception, doomed from its beginning to despair?

He had risen in order to put a little space between him and his task, for physical distance would often result in improved perspective, a wider view of his material and a better chance of conspectus. Yes, the mere feeling of relief on turning away from the battlefield had been known to work like an inspiration. And a more innocent one than that purveyed by alcohol or strong, black coffee.

The little cup stood on the side-table. Perhaps it would help him out of the impasse? No, no, not again! Not the doctor only, but somebody else too, a more important somebody, had cautioned him against that sort of thing—another person, who lived over in Weimar and for whom he felt a love which was a mixture of hostility and yearning. That was a wise man. He knew how to live and create; did not abuse himself; was full of self-regard.

Quiet reigned in the house. There was only the wind, driving down the Schlossgasse and dashing the rain in gusts against the panes. They were all asleep—the landlord and his family, Lotte and the children. And here he stood by the cold stove, awake, alone, tormented; blinking across at the work in which his morbid self-dissatisfaction would not let him believe.

His neck rose long and white out of his stock and his knock-kneed legs showed between the skirts of his dressing-gown. The red hair was smoothed back from a thin, high forehead; it retreated in bays from his veined white temples and hung down in thin locks over the ears. His nose was aquiline, with an abrupt whitish tip; above it the well-marked line of the brows almost met. They were darker than his hair, and gave the deep-set, inflamed eyes a tragic, staring look. He could not breathe through his nose; so he opened his thin lips, and made the freckled, sickly cheeks look even more sunken thereby.

No, it was a failure, it was all hopelessly wrong. The

army ought to have been brought in! The army was the root of the whole thing. But it was impossible to present it before the eyes of the audience—and was art powerful enough thus to enforce the imagination? Besides, his hero was no hero; he was contemptible, he was frigid. The situation was wrong, the language was wrong; it was a dry pedestrian lecture, good for a history class but as drama absolutely hopeless!

Very good, then, it was over. A defeat. A failure. Bankruptcy. He would write to Körner, the good Körner, who believed in him, who clung with childlike faith to his genius. He would scoff, scold, beseech—this friend of his; would remind him of the *Carlos,* which likewise had issued out of doubts and pains and rewritings and after all the anguish turned out to be something really fine, a genuine masterpiece. But times were changed. Then he had been a man still capable of taking a strong, confident grip on a thing and giving it triumphant shape. Doubts and struggles? Yes. And ill he had been, perhaps more ill than now; a fugitive, oppressed and hungry, at odds with the world, humanly speaking a beggar. But young, still young! Each time, however low he had sunk, his resilient spirit had leaped up anew; upon the hour of affliction had followed the feeling of triumphant self-confidence. That came no more, or hardly ever, now. There might be one night of glowing exaltation—when the fires of his genius lighted up an impassioned vision of all that he might do if only they burned on; but it had always to be paid for with a week of enervation and gloom. Faith in the future, his guiding star in times of stress, was dead. Here was the despairing truth: the years of need and nothingness, which he had thought of as the painful testing time, turned out to have been the rich and fruitful ones; and now that a little happiness had fallen to his lot, now that he had ceased to be an intellectual free-booter, and occupied a position of civic dignity, with office and honors, wife and children—now he was exhausted, worn out. To give up, to own himself beaten—that was all there was left to do. He groaned; he pressed his hands to his eyes and dashed up and down the room like one possessed. What he had just thought was so frightful that he could not stand still on the spot where he had thought it. He sat down on a chair by the further wall and stared gloomily at the floor, his clasped hands hanging down between his knees.

His conscience ... how loudly his conscience cried out! He had sinned, sinned against himself all these years, against the delicate instrument that was his body. Those youthful excesses, the nights without sleep, the days spent in close, smoke-laden air, straining his mind and heedless of his body; the narcotics with which he had spurred himself on—all that was now taking its revenge.

And if it did—then he would defy the gods, who decreed the guilt and then imposed the penalties. He had lived as he had to live, he had not had time to be wise, not time to be careful. Here in this place in his chest, when he breathed, coughed, yawned, always in the same spot came this pain, this piercing, stabbing, diabolical little warning; it never left him, since that time in Erfurt five years ago, when he had catarrhal fever and inflammation of the lungs. What was it warning him of? Ah, he knew only too well what it meant—no matter how the doctor chose to put him off. He had no time to be wise and spare himself, no time to save his strength by submission to moral laws. What he wanted to do he must do soon, do quickly, do today.

And the moral laws? . . . Why was it that precisely sin, surrender to the harmful and the consuming, actually seemed to him more moral than any amount of wisdom and frigid self-discipline? Not that constituted morality: not the contemptible knack of keeping a good conscience —rather the struggle and compulsion, the passion and pain.

Pain . . . how his breast swelled at the word! He drew himself up and folded his arms; his gaze, beneath the close-set auburn brows, was kindled by the nobility of his suffering. No man was utterly wretched, so long as he could still speak of his misery in high-sounding and noble words. One thing only was indispensable; the courage to call his life by large and fine names. Not to ascribe his sufferings to bad air and constipation; to be well enough to cherish emotions, to scorn and ignore the material. Just on this one point to be naïve, though in all else sophisticated. To believe, to have strength to believe, in suffering. . . . But he *did* believe in it; so profoundly, so ardently, that nothing which came to pass with suffering could seem to him either useless or evil. His glance sought the manuscript and his arms tightened across his chest. Talent itself—was that not suffering? And if the manuscript over there, his unhappy effort, made him suffer, was not that quite as it should be—a good sign, so to speak? His talents had never been of the copious, ebullient sort; were they to become so he would feel mistrustful. That only happened with beginners and bunglers, with the ignorant and easily satisfied, whose life was not shaped and disciplined by the possession of a gift. For a gift, my friends down there in the audience, a gift is not anything simple, not anything to play with; it is not mere ability. At bottom it is a compulsion; a critical knowledge of the ideal, a permanent dissatisfaction, which rises only through suffering to the height of its powers. And it is to the greatest, the most unsatisfied, that their gift is the sharpest scourge. Not to complain, not to boast; to think modestly, patiently of one's pain; and if not a day in the week, not even an hour, be free from it—what then? To make light and little of it all, of suffering and achievement alike—that was what made a man great.

He stood up, pulled out his snuff-box and sniffed eagerly, then suddenly clasped his hands behind his back and strode so briskly through the room that the flames of the candles flickered in the draught. Greatness, distinction, world conquest and an imperishable name! To be happy and unknown, what was that by comparison? To be known—known and loved by all the world—ah, they might call that egotism, those who knew naught of the urge, naught of the sweetness of this dream! Everything out of the ordinary is egotistic, in proportion to its suffering. "Speak for yourselves," it says, "ye without mission on this earth, ye whose life is so much easier than mine!" And Ambition says: "Shall my sufferings be vain? No, they must make me great!"

The nostrils of his great nose dilated, his gaze darted fiercely about the room. His right hand was thrust hard and far into the opening of his dressing-gown, his left arm hung down, the fist clenched. A fugitive red played

in the gaunt cheeks—a glow thrown up from the fire of his artistic egoism: that passion for his own ego, which burnt unquenchably in his being's depths. Well he knew it, the secret intoxication of this love! Sometimes he needed only to contemplate his own hand, to be filled with the liveliest tenderness towards himself, in whose service he was bent on spending all the talent, all the art that he owned. And he was right so to do, there was nothing base about it. For deeper still than his egoism lay the knowledge that he was freely consuming and sacrificing himself in the service of a high ideal, not as a virtue, of course, but rather out of sheer necessity. And this was his ambition: that no one should be greater than he, who had not also suffered more for the sake of the high ideal. No one. He stood still, his hand over his eyes, his body turned aside in a posture of shrinking and avoidance. For already the inevitable thought had stabbed him: the thought of that other man, that radiant being, so sense-endowed, so divinely unconscious, that man over there in Weimar, whom he loved and hated. And once more, as always, in deep disquiet, in feverish haste, there began working within him the inevitable sequence of his thoughts: he must assert and define his own nature, his own art, against that other's. Was that other greater? Wherein, then, and why? If he won, would he have sweated blood to do so? If he lost, would his downfall be a tragic sight? He was no hero, no; a god, perhaps. But it was easier to be a god than a hero. Yes, things were easier for him. He was wise, he was deft, he knew how to distinguish between knowing and creating; perhaps that was why he was so blithe and carefree, such an effortless and gushing spring! But if creation was divine, knowledge was heroic, and he who created in knowledge was hero as well as god.

The will to face difficulties. . . . Did anyone realize what discipline and self-control it cost him to shape a sentence, or follow out a hard train of thought? For after all he was ignorant, undisciplined, a slow, dreamy enthusiast. One of Cæsar's letters was harder to write than the most effective scene—and was it not almost for that very reason higher? From the first rhythmical urge of the inward creative force towards matter, towards the material, towards casting in shape and form—from that to the thought, the image, the word, the line—what a struggle, what a Gethsemane! Everything that he wrote was a marvel of yearning after form, shape, line, body; of yearning after the sunlit world of that other man who had only to open his godlike lips and straightway call the bright unshadowed things he saw by name!

And yet—and despite that other man. Where was there an artist, a poet, like himself? Who like him created out

## A WEARY HOUR

of nothing, out of his own breast? A poem was born as music in his soul, as pure, primitive essence, long before it put on a garment of metaphor from the visible world. History, philosophy, passion were no more than pretexts and vehicles for something which had little to do with them, but was at home in orphic depths. Words and conceptions were keys upon which his art played and made vibrate the hidden strings. No one realized. The good souls praised him, indeed, for the power of feeling with which he struck one note or another. And his favorite note, his final emotional appeal, the great bell upon which he sounded his summons to the highest feasts of the soul —many there were who responded to its sound. Freedom! But in all their exaltation, certainly he meant by the word both more and less than they did. Freedom—what was it? A self-respecting middle-class attitude towards thrones and princes? Surely not that. When one thinks of all that the spirit of man has dared to put into the word! Freedom from what? After all, from what? Perhaps, indeed, even from happiness, from human happiness, that silken bond, that tender, sacred tie. . . .

From happiness. His lips quivered. It was as though his glance turned inward upon himself; slowly his face sank into his hands. . . . He stood by the bed in the next room, where the flowered curtains hung in motionless folds across the window and the lamp shed a bluish light. He bent over the sweet head on the pillow . . . a ringlet of dark hair lay across her cheek that had the paleness of pearl; the childlike lips were open in slumber. "My wife! Beloved, didst thou yield to my yearning and come to me to be my joy? And that thou art. . . . Lie still and sleep; nay, lift not those sweet shadowy lashes and gaze up at me, as sometimes with thy great, dark, questioning, searching eyes. I love thee so! By God I swear it. It is only that sometimes I am tired out, struggling at my self-imposed task, and my feelings will not respond. And I must not be too utterly thine, never utterly happy in thee, for the sake of my mission."

He kissed her, drew away from her pleasant, slumbrous warmth, looked about him, turned back to the outer room. The clock struck; it warned him that the night was already far spent; but likewise it seemed to be mildly marking the end of a weary hour. He drew a deep breath, his lips closed firmly: he went back and took up his pen. No, he must not brood, he was too far down for that. He must not descend into chaos; or at least he must not stop there. Rather out of chaos, which is fulness, he must draw up to the light whatever he found there fit and ripe for form. No brooding! Work! Define, eliminate, fashion, complete!

## A WEARY HOUR

And complete it he did, that effort of a laboring hour. He brought it to an end, perhaps not to a good end, but in any case to an end. And being once finished, lo, it was also good. And from his soul, from music and idea, new works struggled upward to birth, and taking shape gave out light and sound, ringing and shimmering, and giving hint of their infinite origin—as in a shell we hear the sighing of the sea whence it came.

ST. MARY'S COLLEGE OF MARYLAND 48045
ST. MARY'S CITY, MARYLAND